This
Little Princess Story
belongs to:

. . . .

To Lola, Justine, Charlotte, Steph and Clean Cat

First published in Great Britain in 2011 by Andersen Press Ltd.,
20 Vauxhall Bridge Road, London SW1V 2SA.
This paperback edition first published in 2010 by Andersen Press Ltd.
Published in Australia by Random House Australia Pty.,
Level 3, 100 Pacific Highway, North Sydney, NSW 2060.
Text and illustrations copyright © Tony Ross, 2010.
The rights of Tony Ross to be identified as the author and illustrator of this work have
been asserted by them in accordance with the Copyright, Designs and Patents Act, 1988.
All rights reserved. Colour separated in Switzerland by Photolitho AG, Zürich.
Printed and bound in China by Foshan Zhao Rong Printing Co., Ltd.
Tony Ross has used pen, ink and watercolours in this book.

10   9   8   7   6   5   4   3   2   1

British Library Cataloguing in Publication Data available.

ISBN 978 1 84270 222 2 (Trade Paperback edition)
ISBN 978 1 78344 024 5 (Riverside edition)

A Little Princess Story

I Want to
Do It by Myself!

Tony Ross

Andersen Press

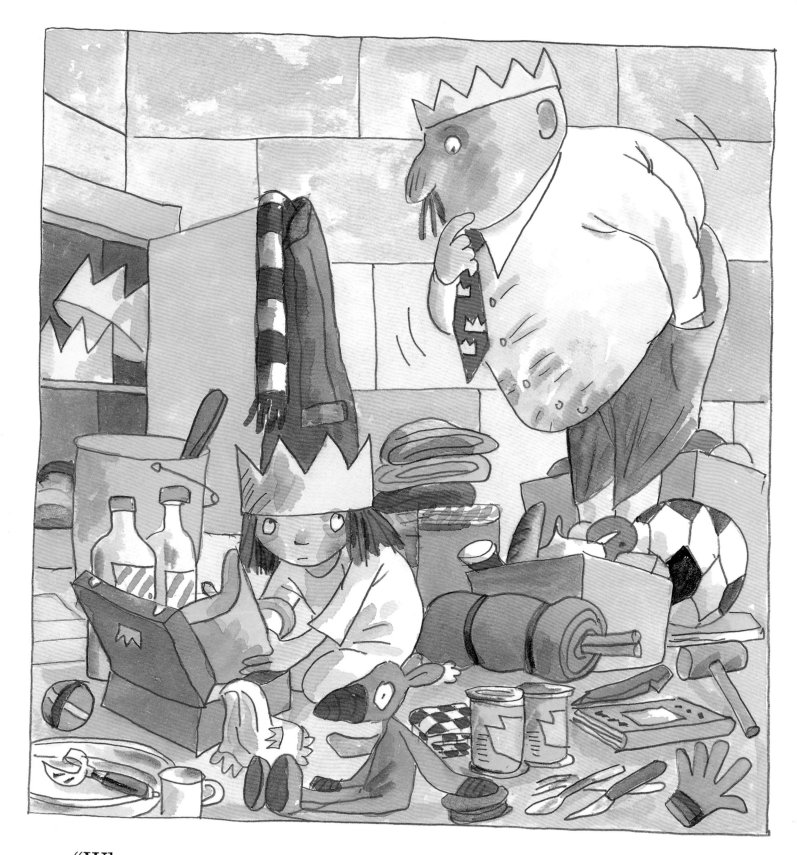

"Where are you going, Little Princess?" asked the King.
"I'm going camping," said the Little Princess.

"Let me carry your bags, then," said the Queen.
"No!" said the Little Princess. "I want to do it by myself!"

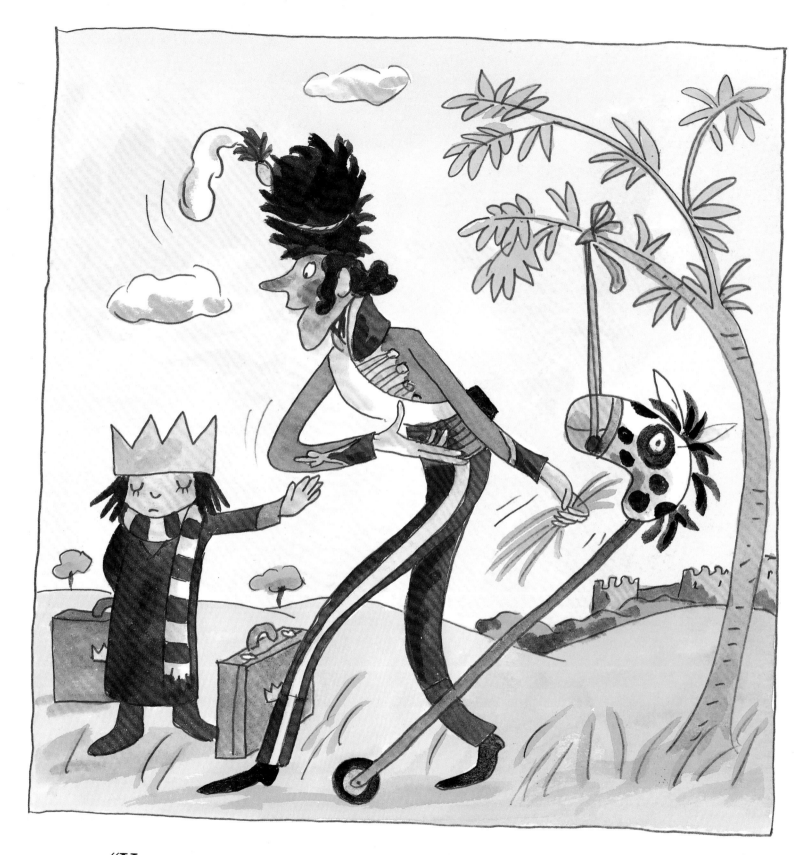

"You can go on my horse!" suggested the General.
"No!" said the Little Princess. "I want to do it by myself!"

"My boats will help to take your bags," said the Admiral.
"No!" said the Little Princess. "I want to do it by myself!"

And so, the Little Princess set off, all by herself . . .
. . . and soon found a beautiful place to camp.

But when she looked in her bags, she found that she
had forgotten to bring her tent.

So when the Little Princess went off to find something to use as a tent, the Prime Minister secretly set up his for her.

"Oh bother!" said the Little Princess when she returned.
"I must have brought a tent after all. I am SO forgetful.
I think I will make supper."

But when she looked in her bags, she found that she
had forgotten a tin opener. She had forgotten a tin
as well, so she went to look for something to eat.

While she was away, the Cook made a wonderful supper ready for her return. Although she could not remember making it, it was very tasty.

"Time for bed!" the Little Princess thought.
But she had forgotten to bring a blanket and a pillow.
While she was away, looking for something to sleep on . . .

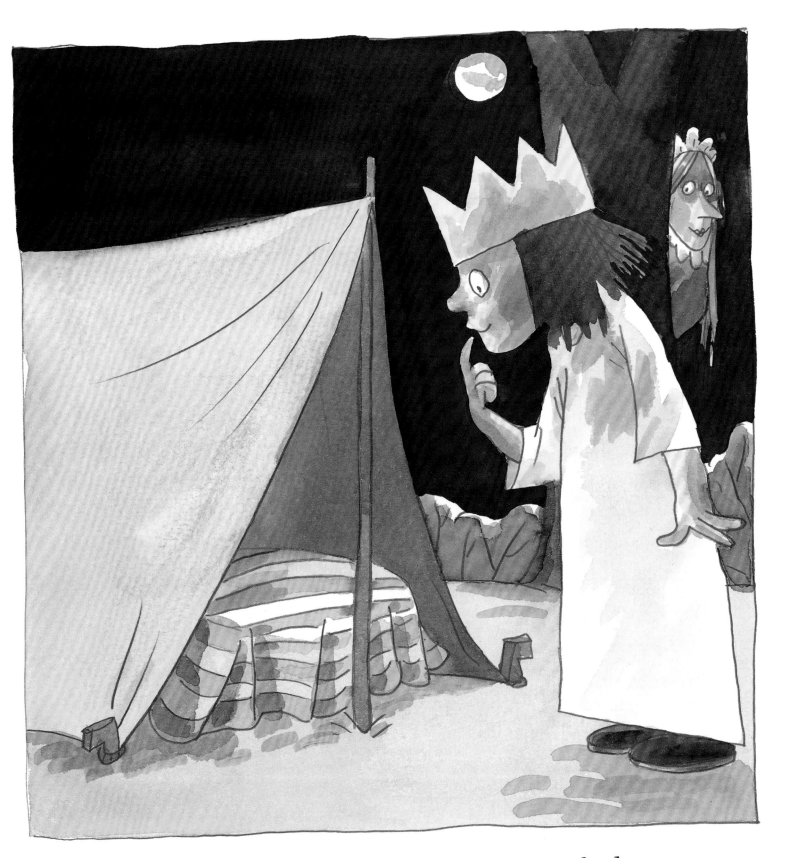

. . . the Maid made up a lovely camp bed.
"Oh BODDLE!" said the Little Princess. "I must
have forgotten I had that."

So the Little Princess tumbled into bed, and fell into a happy sleep. She would have cuddled Gilbert, if she had remembered to bring him.

In the morning, she looked in her bag for her towel and toothbrush, but she had forgotten to bring them.

Then she spotted them, under a bush.
"I must have put them there in my sleep!" she said.

After her wash, she sat down, to think of something to do.

As there was NOTHING to do, the Little Princess packed her bags again and set off home.

"Funny," she thought, "these bags seem heavier than they were yesterday. My stuff must have grown."

On the way back, she met the Gardener.
"Shall I help you with those heavy bags?" he said.

"NO, thanks!" said the Little Princess.
"I want to do it by myself!"

When she got home, everyone met her at the gate.
"How was your camping holiday?" they asked.

"It was WONDERFUL!" said the Little Princess.
"But I am tired now, because . . .

. . . I DID IT ALL BY MYSELF!"

Other Little Princess Books

I Didn't Do it!

I Don't Want to Go to Hospital!

I Don't Want to Wash My Hands!

I Want a Boyfriend!

I Want a Party!

I Want a Sister!

I Want My Dummy!

I Want My Light On!

I Want My Potty!

I Want to Be!

I Want to Do it By Myself!

I Want to Go Home!

I Want to Win!

I Want Two Birthdays!

Little Princess titles are also available as eBooks.

LITTLE PRINCESS TV TIE-INS

Fun in the Sun!

I Want to Do Magic!

I Want My Sledge!

I Don't Like Salad!

I Don't Want to Comb My Hair!

I Want to Go to the Fair!

I Want to Be a Cavegirl!

I Want to Be Tall!

I Want My Sledge! Book and DVD